W9-BRC-554

Caillou

Happy Halloween

Adaptation of the original text by Francine Allen, based on the animated series
Illustrations taken from the animated series and adapted by Eric Sévigny

Caillou had been looking forward to dressing up, and now it was finally Halloween!
Mommy had made him an astronaut costume. She helped him put it on. Daddy came in with Caillou's helmet. "So, little spaceman, are you ready for takeoff?" Daddy asked.
"Almost, Daddy!" Caillou answered.

"Look, Rosie!" Mommy said. "Here's your clown costume, just like you wanted."

Rosie saw the clown costume, and suddenly she didn't want to dress up and go out.

"No," Rosie said.

"You don't want to go trick-or-treating?" Mommy asked.

"No!" Rosie said.

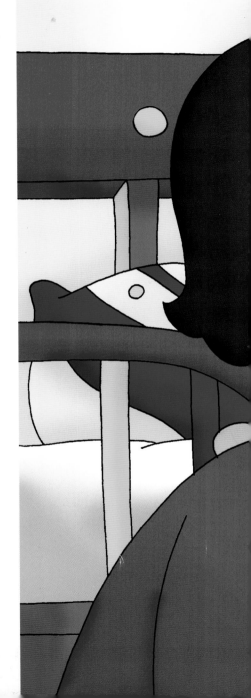

Caillou was really surprised. He didn't know that the clown costume reminded Rosie of how she used to be afraid of clowns.

"Maybe Rosie's scared to go out trick-or-treating," Mommy explained. "I'll stay home with her while you and Daddy go out."

Caillou and Daddy left the house.
It was dark and spooky outside!
There were jack-o'-lanterns everywhere.
Lights flickered in the dark.

"Let's go to Mr. Hinkle's house first,"
Daddy said.
Caillou walked up to Mr. Hinkle's
front door, and Daddy waited at the
foot of the stairs.
"Trick or treat!" Caillou said.

"Hello, there!" Mr. Hinkle said.
"It's not every day I get a visit from an astronaut. What a nice surprise, Caillou!"
Caillou was happy that Mr. Hinkle recognized him.
"Thank you, Mr. Hinkle," he said, as a big handful of candy dropped into his space bag.

Children in all kinds of costumes were running from house to house. Who was that girl dressed up as a nurse? And who was the Frankenstein monster she was talking to?
"Look at me, Caillou! I'm a scary monster!" said the boy in the mask.
"And I'm a spaceman," Caillou said.

Caillou turned to Daddy and whispered, "That monster is Leo! And Clementine's a nurse."
"Look at all my treats!" Clementine said, showing Leo and Caillou her big bag full of candy.
"Wow, that's a lot!" exclaimed her friends.

Caillou, Leo, and Clementine decided to go to the rest of the houses together. "Trick or treat!" they all shouted. They collected lots of treats, and soon their bags were full of goodies. "It's time to go home now," Daddy said. "Oh, no! Not yet!" Caillou moaned.

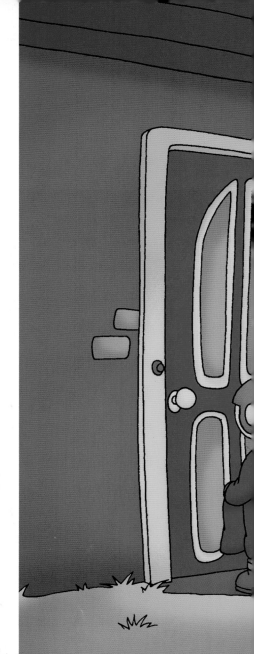

Halloween was almost over, but there was one more doorbell to ring. Caillou, Clementine, and Leo walked up the steps to the front door of Caillou's house.

"Trick or treat!" they shouted one last time.

"Who do we have here? An astronaut, a monster, and a nurse," Mommy said.
Rosie was a little frightened.
"Rosie, it's me!" Caillou said.
"Caillou!" Rosie said, taking off Caillou's space helmet.
"And it's me, too," Leo shouted from behind his mask.
Rosie started giggling. She wasn't afraid of dressing up any more.
"Halloween, yay!"

© 2012 Chouette Publishing (1987) Inc. and Cookie Jar Entertainment Inc.
All rights reserved. The translation or reproduction of any excerpt of this book in any
manner whatsoever, either electronically or mechanically and, more specifically,
by photocopy and/or microfilm, is forbidden.

CAILLOU is a registered trademark of Chouette Publishing (1987) Inc.

Text adapted by Francine Allen based on the scenario of the CAILLOU animated film series
produced by Cookie Jar Entertainment Inc. (© 1997 CINAR Productions (2004) Inc.,
a subsidiary of Cookie Jar Entertainment Inc.).
All rights reserved.

Original story written by Matthew Cope.
Original scenario: Caillou loves Halloween, episode #64.
Illustrations taken from the television series CAILLOU and adapted by Eric Sévigny.
Art Direction: Monique Dupras

The PBS KIDS logo is a registered mark of PBS and is used with permission.

We acknowledge the financial support of the Government of Canada through
the Canada Book Fund for our publishing activities.

Canadian Patrimoine
Heritage canadien

We acknowledge the support of the Ministry of Culture and Communications
of Quebec and SODEC for the publication and promotion of this book.

SODEC
Québec

Bibliothèque et Archives nationales du Québec and
Library and Archives Canada cataloguing in publication

Allen, Francine, 1955-
Caillou: happy Halloween!
2nd ed.
(Clubhouse)
Translation of: Caillou se déguise.
For children aged 3 and up.

ISBN 978-2-89450-932-6

1. Halloween - Juvenile literature. 2. Disguise - Juvenile literature. I. Sévigny, Éric.
II. Title. III. Title: Happy Halloween!. IV. Series: Clubhouse.

GT4965.A4413 2012   j394.2646   C2012-940527-2

Printed in Guangdong, China
10 9 8 7 6 5 4 3 2 1   CHO1840 MAY2012